I AM A BABY

Bob Shea

WALKER BOOKS

AND SUBSIDIARIES

LONDON • BOSTON • SYDNEY • AUCKLAND

I am a baby
and I am not sleepy.

For my wife and son

First published 2022 by Walker Books Ltd
87 Vauxhall Walk, London SE11 5HJ

2 4 6 8 10 9 7 5 3 1

© 2022 Bob Shea

The right of Bob Shea to be identified as author and illustrator of this work has been asserted
by him in accordance with the Copyright, Designs and Patents Act 1988

This book has been typeset in Avenir

Printed in China

British Library Cataloguing in Publication Data:
a catalogue record for this book is available from the British Library

ISBN 978-1-5295-0547-4

www.walker.co.uk

I am not sleepy
because I am a baby.

Mummy is sleepy.

Mummy is sleepy
because I am a baby.

Daddy is grumbling.

Daddy is grumbling
because I am a baby.

Kitty is hiding.

Kitty is hiding
because I am a baby.

Puppy is chubby.

Puppy is chubby
because I am a baby.

Basket is empty!

Basket is empty
because I am a baby.

Table is sticky.

Table is sticky
because I am a baby.

Nappy is squishy.

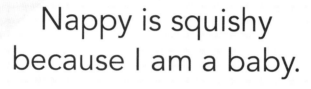

Nappy is squishy
because I am a baby.

Daddy is clumsy.

Daddy is clumsy
because I am a baby.

Mummy is thirsty.

Mummy is thirsty
because I am a baby.

Daddy is stubbly.

Daddy is stubbly
because I am a baby.

Grandma is smiley.

Grandma is smiley
because I am a baby.

Everyone is happy.

Everyone is happy because I am a baby.

I am sleepy.

I am sleepy
because I am a baby.

I am not sleepy.